I0776436

THE MUTE KIDS

Lily Hoàng

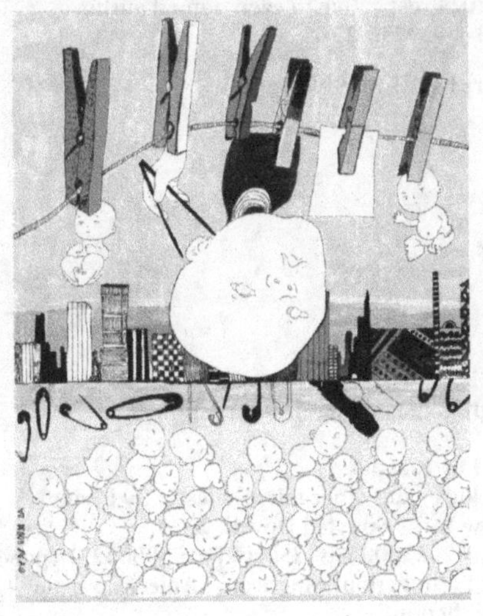

SPUYTEN DUYVIL
New York City

Library of Congress Cataloging-in-Publication Data

Names: Hoang, Lily K., editor.
Title: The mute kids : and other micro-tales / Lily Hoang.
Description: New York : Spuyten Duyvil, 2023.
Identifiers: LCCN 2023000506 | ISBN 9781959556251 (paperback)
Subjects: LCSH: Flash fiction, American. | American fiction--21st century.
 | LCGFT: Flash fiction.
Classification: LCC PS648.F59 M88 2023 | DDC 813/.010806--dc23/eng/20230206
LC record available at https://lccn.loc.gov/2023000506

(from work donated by)

Dan Beachy-Quick
Matt Bell
Dodie Bellamy
Lauren Berlant
Lillian-Yvonne Bertram
Paula Bomer
Amaranth Borsuk
Jenny Boully
Donald Breckenridge
Molly Brodak
Amina Cain
Teresa Carmody
Amy Sara Carroll
Daniel Chand
Alexandra Chasin
Kim Chinquee
Don Mee Choi
Noah Cicero
Joshua Corey
Lucy Corin
Mark Cugini
Cody Dalton
Jeremy M. Davies
Oliver de la Paz
Jereme Dean
Giancarlo DiTrapano

Trevor Dodge
Sandra Doller
Kate Durbin
Danielle Dutton
Cornelius Eady
Elizabeth Earley
Brian Evenson
Extie Ecks
Melissa Febos
Molly Gaudry
Kate Gale
Carmen Giménez
Lara Glenum
Robert Gluck
Noah Eli Gordon
Casey Gray
Richard Greenfield
David Griffith
Stacy Hardy
Rebecca Hazelton
HR Hegnauer
Cathy Park Hong
Greg Howard
Joanna Howard
Frances Hwang
Brenda Iijima
Jac Jemc
Gish Jen

Jeremy Johnson
Shane Jones
Stephen Graham Jones
Tim Jones-Yelvington
Diana Khoi Nguyen
Kevin Killian
Michael Kimball
Amy King
Chris Kraus
Krystal Languell
Evan Lavender-Smith
Evyn Lê Espiritu Ghandi
Yen Lê Espiritu
Janice Lee
Marie Myong-Ok Lee
Dana Levin
Stacey Levine
Tan Lin
Ben Loory
Robert Lopez
Kirsten Lunstrum
François Luong
Lauren Markham
Sara Renee Marshall
J. Michael Martinez
Michael Martone
Scott McClanahan
Joyelle McSweeney

Lincoln Michel
Megan Milks
Lydia Millet
Christina Milletti
Feliz Molina
Dinty W. Moore
Gene Morgan
Fred Moten
Nayomi Munaweera
Michelle Naka Pierce
Sawako Nakayasu
Sianne Ngai
Vi Khi Nao
Viet Thanh Nguyen
Nadxi Nieto
Alissa Nutting
Rodrigo Olavarría
Lance Olsen
Danielle Pafunda
Aimee Parkison
Ted Pelton
Aimee Phan
Li Po
Khadijah Queen
Imad Rahman
Marthe Reed
Wendy Rawlings
Daniel Riordan

Kathleen Rooney
Joanna Ruocco
David Ryan
Kevin Sampsell
Timothy Schaffert
Zachery Schomburg
Michael Seidinger
Aurelie Sheehan
Brandon Shimoda
Katie Jean Shinkle
Sandra Simmonds
Justin Sirois
Abraham Smith
Brandon Som
Amber Sparks
Ken Sparling
Anna Joy Springer
Sampson Starkweather
Michael Stewart
Stephanie Strickland
Dao Strom
Mathias Svalina
Stacey Teague
Roberto Tejada
Daniel Tiffany
Steve Tomasula
Ryan Valdez
Matias Viegener

Jackie Wang
Karen Whitmore
Joel Whitney
Ronaldo Wilson
Joshua Marie Wilkinson
Adam Wilson
Mike Young
Carolyn Zaikowski
&
Jenny Zhang

THE MUTE KIDS
(micro-tales)

OLD SILVER HAIR – I
(from Kirsten Lunstrum)

In the California king, Old Silver Hair turns her face into pillow's swell. It is too grand. In the queen, Old Silver Hair bucks her skin against the silk sheets. It is too subdued. In the twin, her wicked old feet twitch with disgruntled sleep. It is too petite. As such, when the Three Little Bears return, she is already gone, her belly bulging with unfortunate oatmeal and splinters.

OLD SILVER HAIR – II
(from Lucy Corin)

Theirs was not the most luxurious of bathrooms, but they had three. Old Silver Hair went into the first—clearly Pappa Bear's—and she had to use a step stool to reach the sink. She stretches as substantially as she can and the handle remains too far to negotiate. *Everything is just so high off the ground. Who can reach all that?*, Old Silver Hair says. She shakes her old crone head shiny with polish and pomade. Old Silver Hair moves on to the second bathroom. Vanilla and lavender salts nibble at her paper skin and she looks down at streaks of blood all over her body. *Too damn exfoliating!*, Old Silver Hair declares. She is almost without hope, but her need to piss is quite pressing! Finally, she arrives at the third bathroom. Everything seems to be perfectly sized for her. Nothing stinks of pretty things. She drops her granny panties and sits. Here, she thinks, even the most demanding customer can relax and love themselves in style.

Old Silver Hair – III

(from Brian Awesome)

"The parameters of this bed are all wrong," Old Silver Hair yells out. The room is calm, so she shakes her feet free of her dirty socks, her undomesticated legs flapping feral. This is where the stories are all wrong, call it liberal divergences, call it straight up lies, doesn't matter—you see, Old Silver Hair does not go for the porridge first. She is a napper, a mid-day rester, and she attempts sleep, and upon failing, she pushes her circular body towards the kitchen nook. Sunlight glimmers through the windows, her pupils lasso in tight. Outside, the Three Bears are still walking along the waves, their effrontery paws imprinting the sand. They are unstoppable and fearless: they are bears! Meanwhile, Old Silver Hair has tussled all three beds. She eats all three bowls of porridge. Her hunchback unable to align orthogonally, she pushes the parameters of all three chairs until they collapse, not down but out—an explosion. The Three Bears return and Old Silver Hair is already gone and then all the stories transform Old Silver Hair into Goldilocks and the whole fable becomes a polynomial aberration and this pisses off the Three Bears to this very day.

THE APOCALYPSE
(from Dan Beachy-Quick)

Apocalypse! Too many millennia have passed—of unwelcomed quiet. The sun is a blank syllable, a syllable without light: she is dead. The grass grows and the flowers bloom, but we remain taciturn. Nature acts for us like a mime for children, mimicking motions, but keeping the secret words unknown. We see the dance, but to the melody we find ourselves deaf, guessing at the music by the swaying of stems and branches.

MAGICAL BUNNIES
(from Matt Bell)

"A dollhouse is fed with rabbit fences," the mother says to alarm clock his nightmares. The place of his body is nowhere enough for birds to get it clean: the proclaimed hazard and its nightly shadow: growing bristles, dethroning brambles. Silent, the future is a mistake. The boy leans down, cuts the shadow clean with a paring knife, heroic.

Tea with the Teacher
(from Dodie Bellamy)

In the midst of a hurricane, the Teacher pours the Student tea and says, "My one indulgence." The Student smiles broadly, her solar plexus fluttering. His lips move with an elegance at once feral and controlled. The Student spills her tea; it rains like outside.

Without Cure

(from Lauren Berlant)

The prince will one day become king, and he's a real bruiser! Antipodal to the prince is his younger sister, with her dour pout face. To her, the world is fragile and repair is useless: her father, her brother, with no more valiant princes left to cure them: we are all one mere gesture away from losing. At night, the prince and the princess sustain their fantasies: one playing swords against real life knights, the other making up spaces without hierarchy but full of unicorns. She braids her hair into a coil pinned high on her child head, because she is versed in the ancient skill of utter, abject unraveling.

The Rodmans

(from Lillian-Yvonne Bertram & Karen Whitmore)

My ex-husband's childhood hero was Dennis Rodman: he wanted that Crayola hair, that firm grimace of a clenched jaw after a shot was rejected like a wreck from the basket, the force so great his palm may as well be indented into the ball. But more than all the hero worship, Rodman wanted to be Dennis Rodman because the basketball player always had a team. On victorious nights, his teammates don soft matching flannel onesies, and they sleep in a big pile, like hamsters, everyone snoring in harmonius pitch.

On the Thieving of Organs
(from Paula Bomer)

When waking, he finds it too inconvenient that his torso is chained to the bed. She shrugs, like she doesn't understand his confusion. She opens up a plastic cooler—filled with ice and beer. She clips off the metal lid with a lighter. She drinks until quenched.

The Porn Star - I
(from Jenny Boully)

When someone else enters the scene, the porn star is directed not to notice. She is in her ripe lemon kitchen, baking cookies. Her comeliness brings on his desire, intense and bawdy. He unties her apron, puts his hands on her narrow hips; he grabs into her fat, and red crescents abraid her skin. It's so incredibly boring, but she keeps at it anyways. Because this is what she is paid to do. In porn, everything is exaggerated, except for her beauty.

THE PORN STAR - II
(from Viet Thanh Nguyen)

When fame strikes, the porn star finds her first gray hair. Not in the mirror, as some ordinary woman might, but on the third page of a tabloid, regretfully in full color. This will not be forgiven. The porn star is furious, her agent is furious—if she loses even one job because of this, he fumes—even her ghost memoirist is furious. Some scandals, like divorce, drug addiction, and getting dumped on IG, unfailingly up her allure, but her fans will never forgive the porn star for public aging.

The Porn Star - III
(from Cornelius Eady)

The porn star leans back, activating her core, showing it off, and her French stockings make every man on set shiver. She parts her legs in achingly slow motion, inviting the cameraman in for a close-up. As the camera focuses, doves fly out in a frenzy and bulbs incandesce all at once.

Later, at the dive bar down the street from his apartment, the cameraman's friends don't even want to hear about it.

The Next Round

(from Donald Breckenridge)

"Another round," you say, apologizing to whom: people passing in opposite desires: running out to catch the bus, the man talking on the pay phone—impossible to hear, save his silent frustrated gestures—the mechanic's stained fingers tapping the wooden bar, eager for a refill. A teenage couple starts at it in the corner, his hands eager at her thighs, her fingers straining his hair. The bartender walks by, a bottle of Jameson crooked against her thigh, the tightness of her elbow holding its glass curves. You watch, you don't sip after she pours. You flip the liquid down your throat, wait for anything to wash by. "This one's on me," you say to the mechanic, and she demures, slipping closer by one stool, says, "I can pay for myself," and you say, "That isn't the point," and she says, "That isn't the point, you're right," and she says, "This one's on me. How about that?," and you say, "It ain't right," but the bartender takes the mechanic's money anyways. When she leaves, she doesn't leave a number. Before she leaves, there is no further conversation, which is just fine by you, friendly irrelevant gestures previewed miniature and ignored.

THE CAT
(from Amina Cain)

But the restaurant is one feeling, the cat another. The restaurant is open: no windows or lurid drapery; parsed essentials; linguine beams. The restaurant is balmy: it feels just perfect in here.

In Distress

(from Teresa Carmody)

Marie invited Dominque to the dinner party, because she knew her neighbor would not come. Politeness—in this case—is simple selfishness, a young curmudgeon, parsimonious damsels.

THE RED SHOES

(from Amy Sara Carroll)

He cut off her feet but left the shoes on—so they could keep on two-stepping, so that he could keep on watching. He winked and said, "Clean this up." He was not a malicious man. Quite the opposite, she'd categorize him as kind. He said, "Then, walk on. You asked for this, remember that." She took off her shirt and ripped it half and fashioned herself a pair of bandage shoes—also red. She saturated a sponge with her blood and rang it out over a bucket. She did this many times, but she looked up only once to watch her feet tango against the horizon. She let out a hearty laugh, almost a delighted snort, and kept on scrubbing.

SOMETHING BORROWED

(from Kim Chinquee)

When she got back to the hotel, the lights were muted. She thought he looked like her in the shadows, only broader and with an unruly beard.

The Reduction of Hills
(from Don Mee Choi)

Between and until, the dendrochronologist solicits trees with an upturned thigh and cable knit stocking, wires encircling, perfectly. The bark hides buttons and ringspots, and the dendrochronologist counts the receipts of time. The mountains are reduced to hills, bombers laborious—but the rings are hearty versus abandon, the trees counter tautology: we are aging, retireless aging, in epochs instead of minutes.

Empty Boards

(from Noah Cicero)

On a tour bus through Cambodia, the guide says we are stopping by a haunted prison. We are warned it is scary, but I am not scared. When we arrive, it is not a prison at all but a concentration camp: blood still slammed against the concrete walls; empty waterboards; machetes and chains and steel spiked collars laid out in front of vacated beds. On the way back, we stop at the Temple of 10,000 Skulls, stacked to epic pyramid heights. We light an incense and I see an American couple. They shake their heads like they understand atrocity. The man says, "I have blue eyes." The woman says, "Why are people torturing me?"

The Land of Rising Seas

(from Joshua Corey)

Here in the land of rising seas—if seas can be called *land*—our expedition is doomed. We find paradise and it is polar and Harry Lime dies one day later and resurrects in three and is dead again before the week is over. This is not a good tiding for us: the ocean is unforgiving and vain. "Pissy Poseidon," we yell out, our distinctive voices surging to singularity, even dead Harry Lime lets his cackle join ours, but not a one of us believes in those old gods, "bring on your mermaids, bring on your sirens." We say this but we are frightened. We are all frightened invisible. Call us Noman! We hope our frozen translucence will save us.

The Professional

(from Mark Cugini)

Another man closes my palm around his open secret. It is truly awful. I am not a priest. I am not an honest man. I know quite enough about being terrible—perhaps that's why he pulls me tender.

THE FALL – I
(from Cody D. Dalton)

Suited with rolling faces, the two step towards precipice, one gesture splitting into the next. Their hands release a melody that determines a fall so graceful they may as well be dreaming.

THE FALL – II

(from Kate Durbin)

Dirt splinters at my toes. The shot switches to wide,
still panning, and it spins twice, the Hollywood
sign visible against the distant mountain.
I eat all the drugs, one at time without water.
Eager, I wait.

The Fall – III
(from Lincoln Michel)

We are out of the spontaneous woods now but we are still running. We are running as though the forest might appear again, and we are deep into rows of corn that tower over forgotten cars. A redwood shrunken to a single stalk, leaves into ears, and we are listening for the rumble of a bending ground. Everything is shrinking, even the horizon is smaller: we fall into the land.

The Fall – IV

(from Carolyn Zaikowski)

Tell me with your dull sickle: What's akin to the brink? Sly against the willows, you fall forward, breaking lines of leaves, and I am broken too. My hand grows along the brink, but you are my champion of the border, the sullied and broad. You made our door of homes crossing into each other's homes, a tender advocate of intersections. You are my actual border, crayola raised against my skin, and although you have built me a door, you will not cross into its threshold—let me tell you: I'm not sure at all.

THE LEECH – I
(from Jeremy M. Davies)

Rudimentary points of conveyance, Victor's nonsense forced itself into a magnetic fluid, one used to exorcise the frog from the princess. He is a leech, a vampire with perfidious fabrications. Staked, nobody liked him anyways.

The Leech – II

(from Abraham Smith)

He is a leech for beauty, halting at each petal to eat in its aroma. He walks away, and each flower is emptied of its smell.

The Labyrinth of Wild Flowers
(from Oliver de la Paz)

The labyrinth has wild flowers crawling out of orbits, and there is a prisoner in this labyrinth. His little boy toes are eager in his sandals. There are no ants in the labyrinth, so he is not scared. Sometimes, the labyrinth talks to the boy in crazy promises: release, respite, resurrection, but the good boy is in a momentary apple blossom, its endearing opulence; he puts his nose against its velveteen leaves. But the little boy has a secret: he never wants to find the exit. He never wants to leave.

The Stranger
(from Giancarlo DiTrapano)

The stranger is dressed casually: unpleated slacks, easy polo, loafers. He could belong in a catalogue. The stranger wants dick and hard. He wants the most beautiful dick in the city, he wants a fake address, he wants to be hurtled, he wants to be on his way to a man who's been waiting for years and years for him to arrive.

INOCULATION
(from Danielle Dutton)

The broken fog was London without falling down. Quiet water tripped at their ankles, the little birds flew past them. Tomorrow, when the allure becomes resistant, ignorance detains desire, and they stay: their pruning feet, together.

The Unbroken Body Throws a Party
(from Elizabeth Earley)

The unbroken body is throwing the party tonight. Doors open in thirty minutes, but since she knows her friends, she won't freak out if there's no one there for at least an hour. If it's still just her own unbroken body sitting alone tucked in a corner after two hours, then there will be a major problem. She's not going to worry about that now though. No preemptive worrying, that's her new motto. She went with fruit bouquets, cheese puffs, and baby back ribs. She was too ambivalent about bread genre, so if anyone asks, she's going to say something sassy about gluten or carbs or raw foods. She's ambivalent about that, too. A few years ago, she'd go for a sourdough ciabatta, no question about it, but these days, she doesn't think she could respect anyone who still had enthusiasm for sourdough, even ironically. The unbroken body doesn't care about nutrition trends, but her body is unbroken and she has no intention of breaking it herself. She's careful with it, but not neurotic. Yesterday, she almost bought a fondue set, but the unbroken body only purchases things that have more than one function, and the capacity to melt two different substances is basically still just one action, and she couldn't even do—more like: *couldn't even fondoo*, she chuckles, because the unbroken body is the type of body that chuckles when amused—both at the same time, no, she'd have to: 1. use, 2. wash, and 3. dry, before she could use it again. And if the unbroken body knows herself, and she does, duh, she would only ever use a fondue set once. She can already imagine it: she buys the fondue set and goes all out hedonist with the soft cheeses and vascular chocolates. She splurges on the sticks with the pretty engravings in the handle, or maybe just the ones with a really cute handle, and exotic island fruits and whatever else people on the Internet recommend as edible dipping instrument. At the party, it's a huge, huge success. Everyone loves the fondue. Steph and Paul have one, and they're so embarrassed that they've never taken it out of the box— gasp! If only they'd known! No one else has their own fondue set, and two of the unbroken body's less discreet friends ask her how much one of these runs but the unbroken body has got too much class to go throwing out a number like that. The unbroken body says that she must've bought it a less than ideal time, but already, she knows it's worth every penny. As she says it, she will know that she doesn't believe it. She will be lying. To her friends. If one doesn't lie to her friends, who is she supposed to lie to? Although the fondue smashes all box office records, the unbroken body will never use it again. And, if she owns it and doesn't use it, she'll feel guilt and shame about not putting it to good use, which will mean that she definitely won't be using it for another year or two, and in another year or two, when the opportunity arises, she won't use it again, and so functions a cycle. That's what a cycle does. The invitations say 7:30pm, and it's nearly that golden hour. The hour is, in fact, literally golden because she has gold streamers and gold plasticware and shiny gold plates and cheese puffs to sit atop them. She turns on the soft gold fairy lights. Boy, it's been an active day. Now, it needs a moment to collect itself, and the unbroken body apologizes to her body because the night is sure to be a non-memorable one, as in, one she won't remember and that's most likely going to save her from a week of apologies and embarrassment. Better not to remember such unfortunate moments in one's life. She changes the playlist from "Ohx4 Staying Alive" to "Carnival Cowboy Nights" and that is *not* the one, scrolls down, pauses the screen, scrolls down more, then lithely up, the epiphany hits, lands on quite the fetching little diddy, and she does say so herself, "Dance Body Dance #7." As if right on cue, her friends knock in time with the bass drum and the unbroken body throws itself into hugs and more hugs, with all her friends, a celebration for no particular reason but its own insubordination.

The Punish
(from Brian Evenson)

We use the verb as a noun because he is stupid—and not very funny. We give him a dummy name because he is a dummy. We want to throw penis jokes at him, but he wouldn't get them anyways. We slap at his face because this is what The Punish deserves: punishment.

A Bucket List Diary Entry
(from Molly Gaudry)

Last time, the dog drowned, so I crawled into the reservoir and pulled his body free. He wasn't my dog, but he was a good dog, I could tell. I pet his dead dog head, as if that might offer even more relief than being dead already does.

The Tart

(from Carmen Giménez)

Her big fat mouth held onto a morning cloud; it kissed her a million oceanic kisses, which she drank—like blood—like a big sour cherry slurpee.

THE DEAD
(from Robert Gluck)

I find Ed's helpless corpse in bed, his jaw slack of human nature. I prepare my eulogy of cached collections: how I told him at our first meeting that the morning was the most appalling time of day; the babble language only we could understand, but not always; that time I cried because the day was no longer mine to give away; the unique imprint of his handwriting, how I would turn over the paper and feel the language blindly. I touch Ed's face, the slow slope of his arm, his smooth immobile organs—mourning in my mother's voice—calming, distancing.

Ruby Will

(from Noah Eli Gordon)

When Ruby turned six, she made a time capsule with her father. They each wrote two letters, one to the other's future self and one to their own self's future self. Ruby could read and she knew all the different sounds each letter could make, but word composition was still a major challenge. She'd begged her father to act as her private court stenographer, but he said that would ruin the point. He told her about the time capsule he'd made when he was her age, when her grandpapa was alive and just two years older than he was right now. Ruby had never met her grandpapa, but she loved hearing about her daddy's daddy, and she knew that if life had worked out in a different way, they'd be best friends. Ruby tried her best to compose the two letters. It took her forty-three whole minutes to write five sentences to her father, and she beamed at its completion. "I wrote you a whole book, Daddy," she said, and he promised that he couldn't wait to read it. "Then how come you're gonna wait? Do you really have to wait for ten whole years? That's more years than me!"

she said, showing him six fingers and then popping up all her fingers at once. Just as she'd suspected, he told her to be patient. "But you're going to have to practice patience forever and ever." She turned like a ballerina on one tippy-toe and leapt off to write the second letter. Ten minutes later, she cheated and just drew flowers and dinosaurs on the paper and folded it up and crammed it into an envelope, which she licked and pressed. Using a brown crayon, she wrote, "To: Ruby Will, From: Ruby Now." She traced the brown with a dark red, and the letters lost their individuality, becoming one mass of color and wax.

By chance, Ruby's boyfriend took her on a trip to the town she grew up in, almost thirty years later. His plan was to bring her to her old house and propose to her in the backyard. He'd already contacted the current owners, and they strung up some fairy lights in the branches of the old redbud tree, which happened to be flowering, and they even chilled champagne in an ice bucket, which they stashed behind the shed.

She squealed and hugged him, but then she jumped back, smoothed down her dress to collect herself, and told him she'd give him an answer—after they found the time capsule. Her voice was all flirty, and they both knew what her answer would be. She didn't remember where exactly they'd buried it, and he dug way too many holes. The new owners had already been so generous, and he doubted they'd bow to romantic gestures ever again. Billowing callouses pronounced their fresh presence on his fingers and palms. He winced at their burn but did not complain. They dusted the exterior clean, and she tucked the letters her father had penned and the one she'd written to him into her bag, unopened. She knew she would marry him, and their lives would be full of joy and some hardships, but she couldn't share her father with him, not yet. With him, her future husband, she opened the letter she'd written to "Ruby Will." She laughed, "Because Ruby did something in the past and Ruby does something in the present, so Ruby Will—get it?" The letter was mostly misshapen kid art, nothing spectacular, and for a second, she almost felt embarrassed that she'd made her boyfriend—fiancé—go through so much hassle. Then, he moved the paper slightly, and Ruby saw, beneath her drawings, her father's handwriting, faint, as though it had been erased from the page, but still legible. It said: "World's Scariest Things According to Ruby: 1. Fire; 2. Volcanoes; 3. Cartoons with A Narrator."

She couldn't remember if she'd told her father these things or if he'd made this list all on his own. She didn't know why he would've made this list, nor why he'd erased it and then given it to her to write and draw on. There were about ten million more things Ruby wished she could ask her father, too. The ring fit perfectly and the champagne was still cold. They drank it in greedy gulps, and she let out a righteous burp. Later, Ruby will light a fire, stir up a hot chocolate, and read those last three letters. Ruby will find a few answers, but not enough. She will never have enough of her father. And Ruby will acknowledge that all these years later, she is still frightened of the disembodied godlike voice that narrates cartoons. She will wonder if it gets lonely, stuck in a cartoon all by itself, in a world of bright colors and happy voices. The worst kind of loneliness is the one that no one else wants to understand.

THE DOPPLEGANGER

(from Stephen Graham Jones)

If he is a writer, his desire is to be most like Raymond Carver, unbridled sanctuary tracing: he drinks and he drinks, cleans the wax from his ears, empties cupboards of ink cartridges and cigarette remains. He smells his pinky finger and examines the cloudy visqueen.

If he is not a writer, these are not his desires.

Peter Pan
(from Casey Gray)

The mother presses closer to the boy. He wipes his palm against his sweaty scalp. It's too hot, he says, and she says, Do you want to see hot? She shows him videos of weather patterns on her iPhone until he stops pushing her away.

MONSOON

(from Richard Greenfield)

Before there is catastrophe, cartoon raindrops and a violet umbrella neons. I preheat the oven to jeans and a tank—all wrong—and then too fashionable silk shorts and then I am ready for our safari, designer combat boots for show not wear. Richard brings along a flashlight. We are liquid humans, our metal toys, electric forthcomings: he exhausts my laughter, pounces, he is a wonder: information and winding anecdotes—follow the yellow brick road—cleanly alphabetized first by genre. Agora of stories, luminous tragic. Jokes halt if the clouds come too close with their ebon wares, lightning chasers, teaspoon calories. Together, we are refugees, non belongers, locked exterior stage left on a church porch. We count—quiet now: one tomato two tomato three—and there it is, the thunder, just as the icon oracle warned. In India, some college students engineered antirape lingerie, shock currented at rough pressure. Together, we floresce, watch the storm summer on by.

WHAT HAPPENS ON AN UNFAILINGLY CLOUDLESS DAY

(from Stacy Hardy)

It was unfailingly cloudless the day white women fell from the sky. They fell in bunches. Some were clasped to each other, plump velcro skin plus velocity over the force of gravity; others fell alone because they just could not imagine the continuation of their lives without whatever precious thing they desperately held in their arms and legs, be it a yappity dog or an orange Hermes bag, you know the one, or a mink coat. The total value of the jewelry they wore could provide food and shelter to a medium-sized continent for no less than five years. Before then and since then, no single day has ever been so thoroughly analyzed, historicized, or theorized, from politicians to academics to poets, from corporations to prime ministers to religious ministers, too. The only group to not put forth their own spicy take was, of course, white women, having been more or less eliminated as a demographic category. The exact perimeter of the white woman as a demographic category was a debate sub-subject hot enough to cause three civil wars and one nearly successful insurrection. Let's just say that when a man's white mother was no longer available, the consequences were understandably severe. Oh, the suffering! People were determined to hunt down an appropriate moral—whether religious, philosophical, or something else entirely, the road to arrival didn't matter, so long as the end contained as its end a moral—for this historic day, but the end is the end is always ever the end: the day white women fell from the sky was the final day the earth felt peace. Battles broke out with more frequency than a stressed out, hormonal teenager's oily face; after a while, war became so common that they were assigned ISBNs, which was a pretty good strategy for getting people to not care about war. Give it a ten or thirteen digit number in lieu of a distinctive name, and guess who cares? War was so common it was an irrelevant condition of human existence, not unlike the rising temperatures and the rising ocean and the rising cost of living, except for white women, who were all already super dead. An economist, a statistician, and an anthropologist walk into a bar. One asks how much whiteness constitutes white; one is worried about the optics for transgender and gender non-conforming peoples, and to a much lesser extent, this ad nauseum reinforcement of the gender binary; and the other one just wants a fucking beer. A president, the pope, and an environmental activist walk into a bar. One is worried about blocs; one is worried about real estate; and the other just walks out—not enough intoxicants in a bar to make that company endurable! Hey, what's the difference between a punchline and a moral? Eh, the color of meat reflects the quantity of blood in circulation: dark meat is dark because before it was meat, it was maximally used. White meat is chilling poolside. Take, for instance, a chicken. It runs on its thighs, dark, whereas its chest remains flaccid. Take, for instance, a duck. Flight develops its chest dark, whereas its legs can't be bothered. Hard to imagine there was a time when people legitimately thought dumb blondes were a joke. The day white women fell from the sky, all the jokes matured, became these wrinkled, dehydrated old things, and then they, too, died. Without their mommies, men had no model for lust or sublimation; the most rational life partner was one that could be purchased and exchanged, with or without a receipt. Was that the moral? Congress crossed out all the old amendments and left only one: Acts of infallible logic must act in accordance to the phallus. Hey, if you ask for a moral, a moral you shall receive! At the beginning, everyone asked why. But the repeated act of interrogation can cut the human life on average by fifty-two percent. Just think about that next time. Besides, that was a long time ago, and they all lived happily ever after.

THE PROPER UTENSIL

(from Rebecca Hazelton)

Spooned contingencies and forked openings, she stands in the susceptible forest. This is not a place for little girls. Air spears at her skin, so she must decide on her route. Even little girls must choose the proper utensil for danger. She hesitates, spins a bottle, removes from her petticoat one knife after another, as small as a spindle needle, as broad as sound. She is a girl: prepared.

The Trial – I
(from Cathy Park Hong)

Hellswelt, he keels to a ground already cramped with the buried. His fingers wave through the soil, looking for radishes like looking for bones. But instead of the dead, he came back with the living, that limp girl who died seven years back, drowned in the nearly dry river. Brother, we put him on trial and decided he was guilty.

THE TRIAL – II
(from Wendy Rawlings)

We, the bad and the raised, smite and suffocate the Prince. Because he did not kiss her; instead, he killed her. None of it made sense. We shower the Prince with fake fame and then when he is sleeping like a beauty, we put rope around his neck until all his blood stops its movement and he is a disconnected ghost, without body, without harps and angels, but terribly famous: stories will be written about him, about him and his trials against vines and shadowy magic, but they will all be occult lies, ones where he remains the pure hero, loving her truly. But she dies, do you hear us? He kills her and we do not need a trial for him. We know already. And so we pass his judgment into the splinters jutting into his pearl neck.

Anger Management — I
(from Brenda Iijima)

Our animal neverland lacks infrastructure, sure; but, why did the interlocutor have to bid us adieu, wish us a goodnight lovely, spinning off headless as a planet? We step back, let the forthcoming whirlwind open unto he who dares abandon us.

Anger Management - II
(from Nadxi Nieto)

The way he vexes her: some days, she must run outside, bleed her hands against bark, strangle the allergies out of a dogwood tree.

The Comedian
(from Jac Jemc)

To any stranger—crossing the street, bagging our groceries, even taking a piss, or so we assume—Dad's like, Hey, you know I'm a comedian, and sometimes it's a question and other times it's only maybe a question. And if the stranger gives him a dirty look, Dad's like, I can tell a mean joke, and if the stranger doesn't say anything, Dad's like, Nothing beats the high of an audience roaring with laughter, and if the stranger ignores him, Dad's like, I'll be down at the comedy club at eight, maybe nine, and then he scratches his ear, and if the stranger turns and walks away, Dad's like, What's the rush? Are you a Russian?, but he says it like Rush-e-an, and if the stranger punches him in the face, he doesn't even duck. But sometimes, the stranger doesn't ignore him. Sometimes, the stranger asks Dad to tell them more, about being a comedian, because the stranger has always had stage fright and can't fathom such a career choice; the stranger begs Dad to tell them a joke. And that's when he starts laughing. Dad laughs and he laughs and Dad continues to laugh some more. Dad laughs until the stranger has gone far, far away, or at least out of earshot, and that's what's funny: he really is a comedian.

A Restless Night

(from Gish Jen)

Like a cooked shrimp, your arm curls around me.
I push into you, compacted. We do not sleep:
our rinds swim meters along the enchantment of
metronomes.

The Man in the Corner

(from Shane Jones)

And this is how he woke up one day, when he had already learned beauty but only too superficially.

The Mute Kids
(from Kevin Killian)

The girls wear carefully folded pink crepe and the boys wear gilded chiffon. Exterior stage left, they gauze optimism. They are iconic.

HOW HAIR WORKS IN THE REAL WORLD
(from Diana Khoi Nguyen)

While other little kids watch Saturday morning cartoons in their pajamas, the little girl is invested in Chinese martial arts sagas, dubbed into Vietnamese. How else could she understand what they're saying? She prefers the ones with the Chinese translation running along the bottom, and she's pretty sure she will learn Chinese this way. The adults say the ones from Hong Kong are superior, but the little girl can't tell the difference. She doesn't even know where Hong Kong is on a map. Right now, a human-sized condor bird is helping the hero in his darkest hour, and she wishes she had a friend like that. All the actors have long black hair, even the men, but the men fasten most of it into a ball. The little girl can't even figure out how the women's hairdos can happen. So many braids and buns, perfect and gravity resistant, and that's saying something because they're always flying around and jumping to the top of a buildings with one pounce and fighting, too, obviously, but their hair never gets messed up. How do they do it? When her parents ask, the little girl always says she wants to be a doctor when she grows up, because she knows that's what she's supposed to say, but if she had a human-sized condor friend, she'd admit to it that if she could choose something all on her own and if it wouldn't make her parents sad, she would be a hero, just like in the movies. Not an actor in them: she understands the concept of actors. She knows the movies aren't real. It's like a job you go to, like her parents go to a job, and when a character gets hurt, she always worries that the actor will die from it when they get back to the real world. She knows things work differently in the real world that she lives in and the actors live in, because it's not pretend. Like the time Bố got stung by a whole bunch of wasps at work, he came home and the welts were still there, even though he wasn't working anymore. In the movies, someone healthy and strong can transfer their energy into the one who's been beaten up real bad or poisoned, and that's the only way to get better fast. The little girl doesn't understand why her parents want her to be a doctor so bad, when medicine is basically a big waste of time: it's not very effective and almost never saves the day. Once every two weeks, Bố cuts the little girl's hair. She hates this about her life. Heroes don't have short hair, and the little girl is pretty sure her parents understand this rule, too. This is how they keep her here, in this crappy world where she goes to school and nobody talks to her. Nobody picks on her or pushes her around, but they're not nice, either. She knows they're afraid of her because she knows all the killer martial arts moves and if anyone ever tried anything, she knows exactly where to press to make a person freeze in place, which won't kill them or anything, but it's got to be really uncomfortable. She's glad she's never had to use it. Plus, she hates all the tiny hair slivers that she finds spurred into her skin for days and days after. And she hates that every haircut is followed by a trip to the bathtub. The VHS stops before the episode is over. The little girl gets up and presses the rewind button. When it's done, she ejects it and puts it back into the cardboard sleeve. She patters around the house, looking for an adult to put in the next one, quickly, quickly, before she forgets what's going on!

WAITING AT THE BUS STOP
(from Amy King)

We wait at the mouth of the bus stop while other people requiem. The bus passes us by without stopping. And we wait beneath a sky filled with nowhere to go. I place a grass crown against your temples to distance your grace.

Unto Which a Pretty Little Princess is Struck Repeatedly by a Mean Little Girl with Rocks

(from Evan Lavender-Smith)

"Here's one," she says, throwing. "And here's another!" She delivers stone after stone—straight into the pretty little princess's pretty little smock.

To Settle

(from Evyn Lê Espiritu Gandhi)

Equipped with rumors and several styles of contained light—head lamp, torch, flashlight—she arrives from far away. She tries to tell them that she is hungry and cold and too sick to be harmful. They do not share a common language, but only a few days later, she recovers, supple and strong, in possession of a stubborn beauty that strikes. She offers to exchange her advanced technology for a place with them. It's all she's ever wanted, really, to belong in a community, to settle down. She can protect them; she has so many versatile skills. They point at the door, which she understands to mean that she should give them privacy judge her worth. It's all for show. She can't understand two consecutive words they say—quite possibly they're not yet advanced enough to use words in a meaningful way—but she knows they will not refuse her. She coughs, lets out a single catastrophic sneeze, and waits for the colonies to replicate.

THE MAKE-UP MIRROR

(from Yến Lê Espiritu)

When she turned eleven, Mrs. Patterson gave the refugee a gift. The Patterson family, a family of faith, had volunteered to sponsor a family of refugees from Vietnam—about the country itself, Mr. Patterson would rather not say much because his wife had taught him when to speak and when a certain prudence was required, but its non-Communist people were innocent and deserving of charity. The Pattersons were ideologically against war, but they were not the kind of people who go around waving signs and smoking dope, either.

Mrs. Patterson apologized because she'd barely taken the time to wrap it, but she was sure the refugee would be *thrilled* with the gift. She held out a bouquet of newspaper. The refugee shyly picked off each piece of sticky tape without tearing the thin paper, and Mrs. Patterson noted her nimble fingers and thought she'd mature into an excellent seamstress. The refugee uncovered a green square plastic thing, and she put her hands up to her cheeks and squealed, as she'd seen the gesture convey surprise and delight, none of which she felt for this plastic box. Mrs. Patterson felt such satisfaction that her gift had thrilled the refugee girl, just as she'd known it would—and she hadn't even figured out there was anything inside yet. Poor dear, Mrs. Patterson thought, what had she lived through that a plain box would bring her such joy? Mrs. Patterson did not want to think about poverty and bombs, so instead, she took the box and pressed a button. She watched the refugee's revelation with giddy anticipation. The box popped open to reveal a small mirror and compacted powder. Mrs. Patterson explained how to use it. She'd hastily bought her own color, which gave the refugee's face a sickly aura. This disappointed her, but even more of a disappointment was the girl's response. She'd been so grateful for the box, but she didn't seem to care about the make-up itself. Instead, she stared dumbly at her own reflection. She hadn't even properly thanked her. After minutes of silent staring, Mrs. Patterson snapped the compact shut, but the refugee's daze did not abate. She walked her into the Patterson game room, where they had set out three little cots for the children. The parents slept on the foldaway sofa, and Mrs. Patterson was pleased with how neat and tidy her little refugee family was. It's not that she had expected savages, but she'd been warned that they might not be as civilized as Americans. Not her refugee family though! They were mannered and clean, perhaps not to her own family's standards, but she could hardly blame them for that. Sitting with excellent posture on her cot, it hadn't taken her long to figure out how to open the compact, and when Mrs. Patterson left, the girl was once again staring at herself in the mirror. The girl was not particularly attractive, which was exactly what Mrs. Patterson was trying to hint at with the compact—with the Mrs. Patterson trademark polish, politeness, and subtlety, maybe a bit too much, seems the refugee missed the point entirely!—and she silently admonished the refugee's obvious vanity.

But the refugee was not vain. Not at all. It was a magic mirror, a portal, and inside it, the refugee saw the life she would be living if her family had not fled. Over the years, the refugee saw herself age. She watched herself nearly die of a sickness her family could not afford to treat. She watched the anguish of recovery and she counted the hours of assiduous study required to earn the highest marks on exams. She watched herself kiss a boy for the first time and she could almost feel his hand in hers at night. She watched the heartbreak and its melancholy, which her reflection determined would not ruin her study. She watched Lunar New Year celebrations, and she watched her father's death, followed shortly by her mother's. Neither were present at her reflection's wedding. The refugee watched an entire lifetime in that silent mirror, and she mourned her own happy life in America. Much like her reflection, the refugee was an excellent student. They both grew into beauty together. She herself kissed a boy for the first time and she experienced the same despair when it ended. In America, she celebrated the new year with everyone else, on January 1, but she lit incense and set out food on the family alter on the lunar one. Her own parents died much later than her reflection's, and they got to witness not only her wedding but the birth of her two children. They hugged her when she received her doctorate. But long before that, the refugee and her family had stopped being refugees. They were Americans: legally, officially, technically. But she would always be a refugee, she'd made that vow to her reflection, even if nobody could hear her.

Chicken Wire

(from Marie Myong-Ok Lee)

General infantry of the tedium, the men iron and fold and scuff and shine. Their bodies are not yet taut: this is still the beginning: weeks of flattening and scaling; deep water and tear gas; ropes and chicken wire. Later, towards the end, washing GI socks one day and running towards the mortar's whistle, being the hero.

Why Won't He Call Me When I've Left
Like a Hundred Messages I Love Him Soooo
Much I've Left Like a Hundred Messages
and Why Won't He Call Me Back I Love Him
Soooo Much and Why Won't He Call Me
Back When I've Left Like A Hundred—

(from Dana Levin)

And: repeat.

The Two Sisters

(from Stacey Levine)

One sister removes and stores her short lime gloves in the cabinet under the skin next to the Clorox and all-purpose cleaners, and the other sister tumbles through hibernating rooms. They play a familiar game: hide and seek. One sister hides an object; the other sister finds it. But the object is not known. One sister chooses the object; the other sister must gander: she must seek. The sisters, you see, are telepathic, which is lovely for life and miserable for play. The other sister plucks a small embroidered handkerchief from her tiny purse. The one sister shakes her head. The other sister drinks from a daiquiri, not frozen but over ice. The one sister persists her shaking. She shakes so hard she falls down. The other sister laughs, "You and your morbidity!" But the one sister does not respond. She is still. She is practically dead! The other sister opens the one sister's veins and clouds surface, freed. Protective or decorative, where do lost gloves go if not into the dust?

FRENCH KISS
(from Robert Lopez)

I close and look at the mirror and in it myself. I lean in and let the two tongues reflect. And I only want to kiss myself more, good god.

ALL THE POTENTIAL
(from Lauren Markham)

Nearly all the empty houses possess a withered grandeur. "Don't you see all the potential?" the developers ask me. Potential is one of those code words that everyone knows and uses to mean whatever they want, no specificity or parameter required. Potential is vapid; it's got no zest left at all. "No," I say, "can't say that I do." Of course, I buy it anyway, because the wildflowers here are too spectacular to waste.

Plot Points

(from Sara Renee Marshall)

This would-be hurt is illustrious like the sentries of my worried palms. It is not prayer—palm unto palm—but the cramp of fingertips streaming into skin. Even hands worry: they rot. Tomorrow, mine will be your slush, eager for rejection after only two tender words, but the sun finally circles the earth. Then, my angry woman hands conduct the plot of your whole opera.

The Ordinary Woman

(from Scott McClanahan)

She was nothing exceptional: not her hair or her face or her body. Everything about her was fully ordinary. I was married to a woman named Sarah. I was her mean; she was my average.

(from Joyelle McSweeney)

Before thought, no one thought to apply mess. After thought, mess applies and applies to everything.

Buyers' Remorse
(from Feliz Molina)

The first scam they ever bought was their bodies—dysfunctional and bloated. And so they read books and newspapers, refused themselves any nourishment except information. Their hair exfoliated receipts of the things they never bought. Together, they starved.

Getting Off

(from Gene Morgan)

Separated by the universe, we masturbate—together—93 billion light years apart.

THE CROPPING OF BIRDS

(from Fred Moten)

The circle of women abolish quilting: our universal machine of quantum anomalies: the management of our fleshed mechanics. "A family tree cropped of birds is not a family tree," they say, blaming us for our intentional deletions. They speak in metaphors separable from meaning, so we protest their conditions—stitching, stitching.

The Truth about Predicting Weather
(from Nayomi Munaweera)

She closes her eyes down tight, lash against lash, and starts counting in primes, and this is how she knows the monsoon will arrive. She's no fortuneteller, no weather forecaster, she's just another little girl, nothing special, but she's also never been wrong. No one believes her, of course, even though not once has she called wolf without one appearing to blow down a house, but say they did believe her, what did she want them to do? Once, she tried bribing the weather. The rain turned salty that day. She opens a window, peers up: sunshine forever, it seems. She grabs an umbrella and sits in her little rocking chair to rest; she can't see it, but high up above her, the sky smugly smirks, disciplined—but then, when temptation's dazzle becomes an insurmountable lure, it whistles and spits and shakes.

THE UNIFICATION
(from Michelle Naka Pierce)

There was once a border here, and the prince and the princess have united their kingdoms. There is no love in their marriage, simply the movement of maps.

THE WEIGHT

(from Sianne Ngai)

With an intonation of linkage, you activate copper bridges sifted from highways: overpassed encounters tied tightly with bunny ears and rainbow eyelets: affect without: your insubstantial irony doting heavy on me. Suited with concept, cognitive searching for a trauma ambiguous to feeling—which is tired—which is disgust—which is unfathomable—allure me sweet.

THE COUPON THIEF
(from Alissa Nutting)

The man sitting next to me is a star, he's mega, he's stunning. I look at him once and fall asleep. It is the opposite of Sleeping Beauty. He is the Beauty and I am asleep and there will be no kisses—not for me at least and definitely not from him. I don't wake when the flight attendant asks me if I want a free beverage, which of course I would, except that I am asleep. I even have free drink tickets, pre-perforated for convenience. I am always thinking ahead like that. I don't wake when the flight attendant comes around to separate trash from recycling—because that's the kind of airline I fly. I only wake up when the mobs behind me push against the edges of the seats, carry-ons clipping my elbows. I wake up and all of my things are scrambled eggs. I wake up and find I've been robbed of all my drink coupons. But it would be wrong to blame the star: because he is perfection.

A Season of Flowers

(from Rodrigo Olavarría)

She'd been insistent that we could not bring the typical kind of floral arrangement that typical people give to the typical hosts of a typical dinner party. *Is that really who you want to be?* she'd asked, and if I'm being honest here, I have always been the incorrect answer to a rhetorical question. I've never had ambitions that exceed mediocrity, and they were the old-school brand of judgmental Communists. Instead, we brought them seeds for every season, and thus, our names were deleted from the roster of execution. Less than a week later, with neither fertilizer nor pesticide, neon filaments uncurled, ringing against gravity with determination and innocence.

THE MOTHER'S BACKBONE – I

(from Aimee Parkison)

The mother's backbone is a spiral staircase and it helixes against gravity—until the bridge of her bones can no longer hold its own weight.

THE MOTHER'S BACKBONE – II
(from Justin Sirois)

An atomic bomb halves our DNA and then gobbles up the leftovers. We are a helix without teeth, feeling all dumped and lonely yet again. With nothing left to dismantle, we cut at paper, folding staircases into phosphorus—going in and between the slow.

The Argument

(from Li Po)

Your tiger sentences expand like poison lilies, like propaganda. I resist your competition: forgiveness.

The Search Party
(from Imad Rahman)

The parents sent a search party after him and they sought, even though everyone knew it was futile. Some hours later, he would lose himself again and then be found and he would be returned to school and he would date two girls but only half-heartedly and he never let things get past third base even though all the girls wanted him to go further and he would not drink too much but still cram his car into another car and he would watch hovering as his body spun around the merrygoround and he would not be harmed but his friend would and that is a guilt he must sustain and he would apply to every college in the States and he would want to run away but he won't know why and he would go to school in Texas and lose his virginity in New Orleans and lose himself again and not be found this time, the search party having given up a decade past.

The Fate of the Suburban House
(from Kathleen Rooney)

The dead housewife used to live in suburbs, but now she is dead. Her mundane hearth sits inside Christmas ornaments and illegitimate memory. At her funeral, no friends attend. Even in death she is abandoned, lonely, stretched out in a coffin; she does not even look like herself anymore.

Homestead

(from Joanna Ruocco)

Stay with me for ten years and this land will be yours. Let me tremble when the judge sends out his ruling. Leave me without chains or home. You are the fearful face upon which I train my baleful eye—because you are just so beautiful.

The Rat Race
(from David Ryan)

To earn the name *ingeniosus* for her whole entire species, this little rat must prove that she can make up no less than three (three!) totally different disguises within fifteen minutes and without stop. That's the bottom line, ladies and boys (ick!). And I bet she's like not even stressed right now, she's all like *Cover Girl* over here, just challenging the whole freaking system over here, just another day is all, but like way better because this little rat, she's about to be the new regime (well, maybe?, everything rides on today), oh and here she comes, ladies and even boys: Go crazy! Let's give her all the support we have inside of our human bodies! Come on! You know how many humans are *ingeniosus*? Let's—Just one more minute, please? Pretty please. I'll be right down, I promise. Please? OK, fine, OK, I'm coming now—*go*!

THE DEVIL – I
(from Selah Saterstrom)

Up close, the devil is not red. That's only from afar. Right up in his face, we want to get out of the way: he is so handsome, downright gorgeous. Then, we were poor and the grown-ups always wanted us together and corralled—and a great distance from them. *You children are just trouble*, they say. Digging and digging, digging that devil right on up, they're right. In the sizzling daylight, we quarry out dirt and sand, travelling lower into the crust, down towards all that magma, and when we see that resplendent devil, we say, *It's getting hot.* We want to run, but boy o boy, that devil sure knows how to loop you into his herd! And the devil steps closer and smiles.

The Devil – II
(from Michael Seidlinger)

The devil eats truth out of your hand. His tongue is feline and simple. He asks if you have any more, you say you don't, he says that you're dumb. "Stupidhead," he says meanly, like a real bully.

The Devil - III

(from Anna Joy Springer)

Well, I told Tommy to put on his headphones already and he was just starting up some tall excuse when the Devil's laughter shot right out from his Bounty Hunter clean as air and sustained, too. You betcha Tommy and I started digging, but the devil wouldn't stop his laughing. He laughed and we dug and it kept on like that for a while and then there was a sudden silence. We both looked up and we knew our faces were an exact matching pair. We dropped to an easy squat, synchronized—almost like we'd been childhood detectoring brothers and I even forgave him for sleeping with my girlfriend, twice, except the truth is I swiped right on him just the night before—and we dug some more, but this time in quiet. And that's when it happened.

Before that, before everything changed, I got to wondering if it was Tommy the Devil was after or me. I thought about the burden of expectations and scripts and how tired the Devil must be of it all and if I ever met him, I'd ask nicely if I could give him a hug. I thought about alienation and whether or not dogs can see in color and the ocean, too, which I've never seen, unless you count the Gulf of Mexico because it is part of an ocean and contains saltwater, and the size of dinosaur bones. The Devil, I decided, was definitely after Tommy. I decided, additionally, to wear the red skirt on my date with Todd that night, and I wondered if the devil wanted to use Tommy's body as his new body or if he just wanted a toy, and if I were Tommy, which would I hate less? Right then, I felt such tender pity for him—our first home together, the fights, his bad negotiation skills and my avoidance, this could be called happiness—and the pinpointer in my hand kept beeping and beeping.

THE MAN IN THE RED BALLOON
(from Timothy Schaffert)

The man in the red balloon turns off the gas to rise higher. He built the basket himself, braiding wicker by moonlight. During the day, he sewed the envelope with nylon thread. He has planned this trip his entire life. When he was a little boy, an angel flew away and so he ascends.

Doctor Henry Heimlich – I
(from Zachary Schomburg)

This is a true story: Doctor Henry Heimlich is still alive! But Doctor Henry Heimlich is sad. Doctor Henry Heimlich is still a scientist too. Best known for the maneuver that saves chocking lives, now he is the newest of the new avant-garde. Doctor Henry Heimlich's thesis: if you inject an ill body with malaria, it will heal. Specifically, malaria will behead cancer, Lyme's disease, and even AIDS. The conclusion: the scientific community laughed first, then they wanted him terminated, stripped of the title *scientist*. The Red Cross stopped calling it the Heimlich Maneuver, opting instead for *abdominal thrusts*, his name properly erased, as if from shadowy curse of memory. Some days, when he is especially sad, he just goes home and rides his horse, a horse is a horse, of—

Doctor Henry Heimlich – II
(from Ben Loory)

You take tweezers to his open mouth. His noxious breath pivots around your face: you want to squeeze his pores. You lose contact with the tweezers, let the metal fall into the refuse of his intestines. You do not want to save him, but regardless, you gather your arms around his waist, push up against his ribs, you do not save him no matter how hard you thrust your fists against his sternum. You are maybe doing it wrong. You are maybe doing it right. He is choking. He is dying. This is your fault. You reach your palm into his throat and your arm is coated with slime. You withdraw, try again. You reach in with the whole of your determination. His death will not be your fault. You gather his organs around your wrist. From his belly, you extract not improperly chewed food but—a snake!

TELEPHONE

(from Katie Jean Shinkle)

In tomorrow's ebullience, a radioactive telephone line will split, take off, go far off. Under the sunshine, it will not be graceful. It will just dangle around, depressed. It's easiest to bomb things on rumor.

Song from the Bottom of the Earth

(from Sandra Simmons)

Above the half-melted glacier, the floor is always soggy. This is not how he had imagined his successful life as a researcher: ice crystal socks, dead toe nails, coiled up in long underwear and an electric blanket that fizzles and sparks if plugged in for more than twenty-two minutes. It's a science, haha. At night, he can hear the separation of ice. It reminds him of a whale song, the elegy that might escape a whale's enormous mouth when a harpoon plunges three feet shy of her heart. It is not the silence of death; it's the laborious sound of dying, loudly and without reprieve.

Lips Are Made for Kissing

(from Brandon Som)

Three hours into her Burt's Bees Shimmer withdrawal, her tender lips unhooked from her mouth, but not knowing where to go or what to do, they flattened and creased and then they were suddenly a kite. This is not a metaphor: they were translucent paper, curving with desolate breeze, absorbing atmosphere. Far below, the girl re-counted her coins, piled them into lean stacks. Without her lips, her gums were dry and cold and lonesome. Every gas station and grocery store within two miles had banned her. They had her face photocopied in pixelated gray. Her tongue reached out, out of habit, and somewhere in the sky, her lips pouted, as if still commanded by the girl's emotions. And just as her lips understood their freedom, their utter disconnection, remarkably unshackled from the whims of that spoiled little brat, a crow clipped the succulent morsel, so plum and plump, and this is why you must never adorn your lips with color or chemical, lest your lips abandon your face one day to feed a family of crows.

THE MISSING OVEN
(from Ken Sparling)

And Gretel's like, "Where's the oven?" and Hansel's like, "There's no oven here," and Gretel's like, "Of course there's an oven! Haven't you read the book?" and out of nowhere pops the Wicked Old Crone and she's like, "Oooh la la, what have we here?" and Gretel's like, "Bitch, where's your oven?" and she's like, "I traded it in for this here desk," and Gretel's like, "Wicked Old Crone, what can you do with a desk?" and the Wicked Old Crone is like, "Come here and I'll show you." Not seeing any danger in it, Gretel goes over to check out the wares. The Wicked Old Crone pulls out a drawer. She withdraws a postcard from the Grand Canyon. The Wicked Old Crone says, "I'm going on vacation." She points to the postcard. "Here," she says. And Hansel and Gretel start laughing. Gretel pulls out a match, strikes it against the desk, lights the thing on fire. "You should've kept the oven, you old crone!" And the Wicked Old Crone stands straight up and her black witch uniform falls like fingers, like ribbons. She opens her creaky old mouth and gobbles the stupid brats right on up.

Granny's Ears – I
(from Stephanie Strickland)

The Hunter is lured from his task. He is supposed to save Little Red, but where is he? Already the wolf has made stew out of Granny's ears and Little Red has swallowed all the liquid, only the eustachian tubes remain—siphoned granular. The Hunter is destined to save the day, but where can he be? Hurry already! Little Red is precipiced!

But the Woodland Giants offer the Hunter the best toys for pleasure: a top, a mirror, jointed dolls, knucklebone dice, and truth be told: the Hunter is tired of saving little girls and damsels. He gets no honor for it. He gets neither ribbons nor medals. This time, he will let Little Red conquer the Big Bad Wolf herself. He wants no part of her petty saga.

Granny's Ears – II
(from Daniel Tiffany)

The Big Bad Wolf takes Granny's ears and makes a stew of them. The stew is done when Granny's ears are translucent gummy. When Little Red knocks on the door, the Big Bad Wolf opens it, invites her in. The Big Bad Wolf pulls out a chair for her, flutters a napkin across her lap, serves her the stew. Little Red eats and she eats, has thirds even! She puts the Big Bad Wolf's paw in her small hand and they dance—until she pulls a bread knife from her petticoat and slits the Big Bad Wolf right across his throat. Straddling his dead body, she kisses his nose sweetly, says, "I'm going to put you in the Lost & Found. I hope somebody claims you."

Stevie Nicks

(from Mathias Svalina)

anic shells our monosyllabic lips: ovarian. This is the curse of dangerous bodies, Stevie Nicks. Do you like to think about bears as we do, never in sleep and always massive? When we think about bears, Stevie Nicks, they are sublime. Or: sometimes we can hold a single bolt of electricity, its prickling little fire, in our chest, on our throats, our mouths the moon's verisimilitude—widened. Heard the one about how the bearded dragon got its photo taken? Text us when you figure it out 718-986-8295. We're only just kicking around here in the waiting room.

A Very Short Dream

(from Roberto Tejada)

When he is awake, he dreams of swimming in the water towers behind the boulevards and courtyard: the unsanctioned thrill of separating water, his gummy skin washed of color, until he is as clear as filtration. Eureka!

THE MUTE SWAN

(from Matias Viegener)

This mute swan is hardly mute. This mute swan gabs and gabs, like women of the hen sexed: pecking with gossip. The mute swan is alien anyways; it does not belong here.

According to Reuters, after given the cursory intelligence quotient test, the governor of New York has decreed the mute swan an enemy of the state—the state of New York at least—and here comes the compulsory sterilization of the imbecilic again, waterboard the bimbo: well played, Governor!

A CONSTELLATION OF RYANS

(from Jackie Wang)

The sea creatures copy themselves in the sky, their fins and tentacles replicating, precipitous cloning, nothing but recessive mutants. In the sky, the sea creatures hold their breaths, anticipatory invasions, participatory brinks. Above the sea, the world turns into a mirror of itself, and the sea creatures watch, unmoved. The reel unstructures and all that remains is flickering neon, sodium chlorided and incandescent. Deep creatures have an extra cone in their eyes—to variegate yellow into mustard grains.

I Love Eggs A Lot

(from Adam Wilson)

Tiffany and Amber have gained more than a couple pounds. They have gained a ton of pounds, like a whole ton. In the morning, they try to exercise. They walk until their breaths are cubicled. They walk until a single pound is sweat from their tank bodies, and along the way, they sizzle gossip like two eggs fried over easy.

Heat

(from Joshua Marie Wilkinson)

How about this?, you say, the hollow of your punctuation falling in antipodal mounds. My dolorous ankles itch like they want something to be there: sweeping insect legs drinking a Shirley Temple from my unmoisturized skin. This is how you make me feel: dry, thirsty, Solarian. Each button on your shirt is a dangerous flare and I want them all on the ground, domicile. Can you turn the radio back up and close your eyes? I want to show you the secret spoils of the wall, what it shone and what it recasts, saliently.

To Fall Apart

(from Jenny Zhang)

Corybantic, I am so uncontained. I lift my stomach and azure paint sidles free—clean as an aquifer and just as refreshing. I want to gather it in my hands and gulp, but my igneous fingers prove better for filtering than holding. I let the paint waterfall and my body releases the eager brilliance of consumption.

THE END OF SOMETHING TERRIBLE:

ACT 1

The End of Something Terrible – I
(from Ted Pelton)

The snow leapt against the windshield like a lion, attacking my eyes with sparkle. You sat in the passenger seat, one hand screwed to the handle for safety. You should have been driving, but you called yourself a feminist. After we crossed the border into Canada, you screamed at me—for all the wrongs I had wronged you—in all the years of years of our tattered relationship. I remained quiet, as I always did with you, passive and afraid. I wish I had abandoned you then, but it took many more years.

Without you, I search for happiness and find it.

And I do not miss you, not one bit.

THE END OF SOMETHING TERRIBLE – II
(from Jereme Dean)

Even his chest contributes in our *talks*, which are really *arguments*, which is really just him yelling. Quiet, I level my belly flat against the powerful forest of his tautological rage.

THE END OF SOMETHING TERRIBLE – III
(from Ronaldo Wilson)

He says my heart is swollen thick as a pig hock, and this is a really terrible condition. He says it is likely I will die and my body will become a variety of soft cheeses, moist and rotten. He says this is what he hopes will happen to me, and when he goes, I am left like crackers, broken crumbs because he broke me, not because he is gone: about that, I rejoice.

THE END OF SOMETHING TERRIBLE – IV
(from Mike Young)

I adjust the knob to char what is already over.

The End of Something Terrible – V
(from Alexandra Chasin)

Overcommitted to white guilt, my ex-husband distributed my Otherness. I was his relief. But what he did not know was how I stereotyped and objectified and reduced his positionality too, how I techniqued his domination. My ex-husband always hated my sex toys: I still prefer masturbation.

From his mouth comes sound larger than rage, which I cannot afford to resist: our double economy: his wrath is not equal to my fear.

The End of Something Terrible – VII
(from Michael Kimball)

We, like miasma, curdled. You may have tried to acclimate yourself to my body temperature—its solicitous movement through and forward—but that only furthered my distress. I was always the calm against your tornadoes, funnels of monstrous despair; eating, eating.

In the quiet of early dusk, I revert to myself, distant from me, but I feel a torrent eclipse my body: anything is possible when you leave me, forever.

The End of Something Great:

Act 2

The End of Something Great – I
(from Danielle Pafunda)

I break your face apart and find it is filled with fiberglass lawn darts. Your lips fall onto me: the hot coals burn my wrists. They simmer there until my bones are aircraft cables and I want to take you on a trip. I want you to look out the window. Your poprocks eyes spark against the pane. This is the beginning of our fracture.

THE END OF SOMETHING GREAT – II
(from Marthe Reed)

Our parallel bodies fall like water, like love, but this is not what you want. Our trajectory towards decline—amnesiac of time. My polar palette divides the separation of our fields: I am a cardinal, you are a sparrow. You do not respond to my mating chimes, you do not answer. Even the pattern of my beating organs elecits nothing. Your eyes are open: why can't you see me?

THE END OF SOMETHING GREAT – III
(from Amaranth Borsuk)

We glitter from within, lit by systems of exchange. Do you remember our joy? The excess of our gathering—Texas, New Mexico, Colorado, the Grand Canyon, Mexico even—it luminates me. I scintillate in memory, while you recede. We have never been to the ocean: is that why we wilt? I am tired of questions. I am exhausted. Our love was never a rose, except in its decay.

The End of Something Great – IV
(from Vi Khi Nao)

Bent by the bow of lust, I imagine you with her. I imagine her body instead of mine—in your bed sleeping on your chest, then waking and jamming your whole cock deep down in her belly. I do not imagine you two fucking though. I can never see her face, only the swell of her tangerine hair, so much fairer than my shadows. I tell you that I love you, but my words are only clothed in nude.

THE END OF SOMETHING GREAT – V
(from Tim Jones-Yelvington)

Each day, I wear sequins like scabs hot-glued to my skin. Below my encrustations, nothing heals. Bacteria fluoresces on my arms; cancer tremors my blood; you destroy me. The freckles on my shoulders turn into holes: deep, hollow shafts: my body is honeycombed. Take me into your sarcophagus and let us merry together. *Even in Hades*, writes Sappho, *I am with you.*

The End of Something Great - VI
(from Sampson Starkweather)

Engendered with dilemma, we are only just electrons and time. Why should I be trusted? Why should you? Our petty lies portend our collapse, but we have seen our world apocalypse so many times that our remnants become reversed polaroids, hidden blankness, the notness of memory never stood a chance against you and your fickle sleep, my beauty.

The End of Something Great – VII

(from Trevor Dodge)

Even if we had gone to Wal-Mart instead, nothing would have changed. You wouldn't miss me more, and my heartbreak would not be any less bleak. I wanted onomatopoeia with you: BLARM, CHIRP, EEEEK, but you gave me songs instead. Let's go do something fun. Let's hold hands and share more than popcorn and a Coke in the dark. Let's play late night bingo or go whitewater rafting. Let's skydive and let our voices blend on our descent. Let us fall—together this time. This is what I would say to you, but my voice is too distant and imaginary.

THE END OF SOMETHING GREAT – VIII

(from Amber Sparks)

We are only ghosts: I go snow blind from staring at you for too long; you trace my thorny boundaries with scissors; I twist away from you, struggling and too vulnerable—but we have already passed, my love.

THE END OF SOMETHING GREAT - IX
(from Frances Hwang)

Teething with the fright of our displacement, you will not hold my hand. You will not put our skins together. "Can you hear the voices of dead dreamers?" I ask, and in my voice lingers the drugged quality of waves, touching the sand and receding again. We wait for help in this drought: we sit in the wind and avoid contact—until you become a stranger—until you are gone—and the silent remains of brine and flowers wash me clean of you.

The End of Something Great – X
(from Joanna Howard)

On Sundays, we used to make our bodies into glass so we could see the traveling buffet of blood sausages, marbled salt pork, terrine crockery thickly coated in congealed fat, the sparkling red wine of ingestion: dark bread. Our stomachs turned like squirrels hiding in their cozy homes, fearful of the cold. I should have understood this as something other than what it was—our meandering out of us—our dark coats and scarves separating what was already divided.

Now, on Sundays, my body is a spreading napkin across your missing lap; I am reduced to frigid dandruff, smudges, crumbs.

The End of Something Great - XI
(from Sandra Doller)

Maybe we make plans for trips and we always take trips—except for this one. Maybe the hotel looks better in the brochure, maybe the pool does not have a slide, maybe you did not leave me alone this time.

THE END OF SOMETHING GREAT – XII

(from Krystal Languell)

We are not a viable business. We are without profit. In today's market: our plummet.

THE END OF SOMETHING GREAT – XIII

(from Lydia Millet)

No longer young, I become game—waiting for your slaughter. I open up my neck to let your arrow bend through my skin. But I cannot sate you, still.

THE END OF SOMETHING GREAT – XIV
(from Jeremy Johnson)

I don't imagine we'll revisit each other, so I'll tell you this: I am not mostly cured: I am little plates too swollen with porcelain—and when the pitch drops, will you nod off and miss it? Another eight to ten years: that's the tedium of our separation, the seams of my fingers dangling to reach towards yours, herringbone stitching.

The End of Something Great – XV
(from Khadijah Queen)

You cross the walking trail over the bayou as if to brave a pair of foxes; you are a scavenger, in search of me. I am hiding by the water, my body stocked inside a tree trunk. I count the rings and centuries of your regrets, for our future that will never develop into a rainforest landscape, destined instead for deserts and cacti. You will never augment my unreciprocated devotion, and I will continue to hide until you tire of the seek. Curtained, I itch against squirreled acorns and shedded fur, reaching the barometer of quit. You stand next to me, put your hand against the tree, release the sheath of socks and shoes. You land in the low water, fast and chocolate lapis lazuli. I watch. You cry, but it is not for me.

THE END OF SOMETHING GREAT – XVI
(from Dinty W. Moore)

Even now, a half century later, you remember how I pulled out my chair, its steady rasp against the linoleum; how I closed the refrigerator taciturn; how my fork scraped against the plate when I did not like the taste. You recall these things warmly, and of you, I remember the fun and drugs and waste—our wasting off. For you, I am mundane. To me, you are a sunburst.

THE END OF SOMETHING GREAT – XVII

(from Michael Stewart)

Our tranquility is glamorous. We are dressed in black tie bests. My gown brushes the terrain and pixie dust flutters around me. Your shirt is still unbuttoned and you are dashing. I don't know this, but tomorrow portends fatality. But for tonight, in a room of beautiful people, we are reckless and young. We are rich with infatuation. Tomorrow, however, we will be solemn and I will abandon you while you are still sleeping. You will wake and the coldness of my absence will make you cuddle tight against the fanning tornado.

The End of Something Great - XVIII
(from HR Hegnauer)

You took me gambling in a rented convertible and I wasted all your money on slot machines. I am addicted, not to gambling, just addicted, and you are a decadent dessert. You delight me. I savor how you refuse to wake, even when my unclad body covers yours. I luxuriate in moment you close the laptop fullscreened with porn, how you elapse your body into mine and the porn can no longer compare to me. The memory of the muted piano of your voice, making you seem soft and disposed. And then there is the embarrassment of remembering: you, at all.

THE END OF SOMETHING GREAT – XIX
(from Andi Olsen)

Without you, there is only concrete and snow. I live in the desert and you live under humidity and the day I leave you—dissoluting—let my body topple like a crow and my bed dermis sheaths of ice over me in substitution for your fleecing touch.

The End of Something Great - XX

(from Chris Kraus)

Cramped with ineffective dreams, I walk pointless around the suburbs. It is after midnight and the winds eddy—but they do not bring you back. You remain my dissatisfaction.

THE END OF SOMETHING GREAT - XXI
(from Lance Olsen)

—I'm sorry, ok? Brandon? Hello? Are you there? But he already hung up, while I was still midsentence somewhere.

The End of Something Great – XXII
(from J. Michael Martinez)

We used to swim such depths from the shore, our bodies lunging against the sand. At three am, we used to late night bingo until neon pink and tangerine stampers introduced dawn. We used to contaminate our bodies and cashiers would wish us *Be safe* instead of *Have a good day*. They did not thank us and our tasteless insobriety.

Now, I seek the spirant hovering between the silences spread open inside your fists: the abandoned metal shells of your departure.

The End of Something Great – XXIII

(from Megan Milks)

With lust engorging my capillaries, I want to fuck you like latticework constellations, your body creaming acid, disintegrating. I want to clean my body sterile and dip myself into your hostility. You deny me, and all I want is to resuscitate you: until you are mine: again.

THE END OF SOMETHING GREAT - XXIV

(from Daniel Riordan)

Apoplexied, I see you on the most meticulous of levels, the blood in your organs falling down. The nuances of each unclouded cell glows when I look at you—yellow mitochondria, mauve ribosomes. I would make fresh juice for you daily; I would clean your body with sea salt and lavender. I would let you age and die, but your body still guides itself away from me, a long and lonely death.

The End of Something Great – XXV

(from Aurelie Sheehan)

There have been too many funerals lately, namely: ours. I mourn in white and cry liquefied obsidian. I defy elements—the memory of us trumping telluric constitution.

The End of Something Great – XVI
(from Tan Lin)

Your silicate skin, like plastic wrapped wet clay prepared for kneading and throwing, I remember: its give against my touch, the tonality of its earth. Without you, I have no minerals left, my feet floating phantasmic, and so I plunge.

The End of Something Great - XXVII
(from François Luong)

A mirror is not a window, you say, and I watch the movement of the clouds: unhurried, hardly perceptible, not—like the two of us. I ask you for definitions and you say I am your surveillance, watching, containing. But you are the first time I have seen all three dimensions and I am a frame holding you, refusing release.

The End of Something Great - XXVIII
(from Steve Tomasula)

Changing direction, your muscles sweep by me one by one, deftly changing the direction of air. I breathe by design or defect: uneven, unbalanced, despairing. Arabesques of men in their brilliant green gowns surround me, but I can recognize only the form of your face in theirs. They are flocks of parrots—imitations. They are not really flocks of birds nor are they schools of fish; they are the maggoty mosaics foretelling our termination.

The End of Something Great – XXIX

(from Stacey Teague)

When I think of you, it is a fleece blanket crammed up my sinuses. When I think of you, it is a bone corset, tightening. When I think of you, aneurysms weep blood into my spinal cord and braid. When I think of you, it is only what is now, never what was—because that would resemble—bliss.

The End of Something Great - XXX

(from Ryan Valdez)

Being entirely naïve, you do not fall, you do not jump, you do not float: you let me—glitter myself around you. Or, you used to, I remember you used to.

THE END OF SOMETHING GREAT - XXXI
(from Lara Glenum)

I howl like a swan, creaming at convergence. It is a bellow of morphic resonance with my disjoined lung. You do this to me: take off my skin and let it be hung. With you, I am only a mannequin, poorly fitted. I trill your voice, overreach my body onto yours, I ovulate your skeleton and let your language open through my mouth. Without you, I starve and roseate, a mere fountain of electrodes.

The End of Something Great – XXXII
(from Kevin Sampsell)

You partition yourself from conflict. When you do this, I feel around for some little clue in the air between us, but you have taken away all the oxygen. You asphyxiate me.

THE END OF SOMETHING GREAT - XXXIII

(from Christina Milletti)

Molten, I beg you for epexegetics, and you repeat that we are over. My skin flakes over your words. If not for you, I'd be someone new. But: I remain. We remain. Even after you exterminate me.

THE END OF SOMETHING GREAT – XXXIV
(from Brandon Shimoda)

You pour tissue down my spinning heart and I let you. The centripetal force burns away my skin, but I ignore the hurt and place persimmons for you next to the bones in the sink. They are our old bones, drying out in the glass daylight. You gather my head of every matter dividing—sure, here you go, plug and drain all the sap out of me that you can, I will find you a vein—take this love out of me, this sudden break of reverie and ache. This is what I know: it is never the last time. I will see you again, I pray.

The End of Something Great – XXXV
(from Joy Harjo)

The world begins at the kitchen table, only you don't have a kitchen table and my kitchen table is in the sunroom. I do not call it destiny and neither do you. You call it the end and I weep. "No matter what, we must eat to live," I say, and you say, "I'm sorry," and I don't say, "This is it," but that's exactly what I mean.

Of course, I will still see you tomorrow or any day. All you have to do is ask: will you?

The End of Something Great – XXXVI
(from Jen Hofer)

In a parcel to you, I subtract pronouns, sign: Love, Lily. When you peel the stitching, feel the sediment stoppage, its craters. I found a ball gag in your sex toy box once and you have never vortexed me—except when you unswept me, scattered and thrum—except: we are something great again, aren't we? And so I close the container of the end and begin—

THE END OF SOMETHING GREAT – XXXVII
(from Shena McAuliffe)

If your living room is the killing floor, unorigami
my mouth and project its wintery heaps along your
walls, magnify my creases and button—but my view
from far below: o how our new city revels and gleams.
Its semen sparks from above me. It's resplendent, look.

The End of Something Great – XXXVIII

(with Gregory Howard)

It's that my skin breaks out, blights of anxious oil. It's that I am fat. It's that I am too weird. It's that my clothes don't match. It's that I take too many drugs. It's my haircut. It's that I am too crazy. It's that my eyes are not blue enough and I am not white enough, I have too many tattoos. Etcetera: but I am good and true.

Still, I impede this: *amabo | amabis | amabit | amabimus | amabitis | amabunt*.

My language was ancient Greek, though, not Latin.

THE END OF SOMETHING GREAT – XXXIX

(from Matthew Salesses)

Wax and myrrh, let my fingers trace the indentation of your cathedral. When we were great, jubilant doors sprang forth doves and prayers— but: the despairing saint is the only saint I believe in— but: ten hail marys and let my trespasses pull forward the dense curtain. When I scroll trough the moving picture of our end, your green eyes technicolor and glitter until emerald.

THE END OF SOMETHING GREAT – XL
(from Joshua Wheeler)

And so we arrive: hope and rhetoric have been staked, and instead of a heap of ash, a pulpit. We stand, reconstructed and glinting; we are apocalypse survivors, victorious and triumphant. The end of something great, it appears, begins again—repeat.

The End of Something
—It wasn't Actually Great After All:

Act 3

I had confused treachery with fun, mistook betrayal for devotion, such juvenile excuses. Misleading, like how the dark side of the moon isn't dark and a sphere does not take sides.

THE END OF SOMETHING—
IT WASN'T ACTUALLY GREAT AFTER ALL - II
(from Aimee Phan)

I was not slave enough to enter your childhood home, not equal enough, either. You said you could never marry me because everyone in your family is blonde and that's your burden, your responsibility, to maintain. I wouldn't understand. Together in your bathtub, you promised me that you'd always lust for me, more than your future white wife, and you'd gamble it all for me to be your mistress. Funny story: I was still convinced it was love. Not wife material, but I had all the right proportions for a sexy mistress. Even funnier story: next, you married a different Viet girl, and later she read through months and months of your text messages inviting me to a romantic getaway, anywhere, just name the place and you'll book the tickets and the hotel. It was not enough that I declined your preludes. She would never forgive me, for trying to seduce you. She said I was a bad Vietnamese girl, that my parents must be embarrassed of me, that I must be stupid or crazy or both for thinking you would ever choose me over her.

She threatened to blast me on Twitter, to email the dean at my university to get me fired. I didn't laugh at her. I'd felt that desperation, before, with you. I told her that you don't deserve her, that she's so much better than you, that she doesn't deserve your abuse, and she doesn't think you're disgusting, not even a little bit. I remember being in the midst of such enforced delusion, too, and she demanded to know why I maintain communication with you, if you're such a monster, and I couldn't find an honest justification.

I have had four major relationships, and two of them have married a Vietnamese girl next. Three times makes a pattern, before then it's just a coincidence. From now on, I'll be my own sun.

THE END OF SOMETHING—
IT WASN'T ACTUALLY GREAT AFTER ALL - III

(from Molly Brodak)

When I'm ready, I find the sky blueblack and opulently open, with freckles that brighten after too much sun. Not really. Honestly, I don't even remember anything special about the day. It was unremarkable. Even though it marked the first day I'd be without you, nothing noteworthy happened on the day itself. Not what I was wearing, not what I saw on the drive across the state of Texas, not what I talked to my friends about when I got home, not what time I went to sleep, nor how long I slept, nothing about meals, I'm sure my cat did something cute, but I couldn't say with any specificity. Then again, what, exactly, would be worth remembering about that day? I'd thought you were really someone special, too good for the likes of me, and you let me know just how much you agreed with this evaluation, and gracious, it took me way too long to see you. What an embarrassing epiphany. You are exactly and only your veneer, nothing deeper than that. You're not a visionary, I was mistaken, and everyone knew it but me. This was a much worse betrayal than all the cheating, and that was quite painful. Quite so. When I left, I was damaged, but not everything was your fault. I participated, too. I can acknowledge my failures. You never claimed to be anyone except exactly who you are, you didn't mislead me, and in the end, you aren't even important enough for me to remember anything about our end. My brain's real estate is a premium good, but it's a little disappointing that you can't afford anything there. See: I've never needed to feel all the moments, but I'd like to remember some of the important ones, something that marks a development or change in my personhood—and maybe a few of the sleazy ones, too.

The End of Something—
It wasn't Actually Great After All - IV
(from Dao Strom)

The day we met, I had emergency tangled in my hair. I couldn't brush it free, and water frightens me. With no blood in your hands, you braided, conditioned it with spit and cum. I locked your front door to shut off the crying. With you, I didn't need to mourn my dead sister. You maintained my euphoria, a heaping supply of it, every four to six hours, or, as needed—because cost was irrelevant.

A few years ago, I bought a new shampoo. Being a woman can be such a hassle and expensive, too: shampoo, conditioner, leave-in conditioner, de-tangler, product, product, add heat, curl, straighten, wave, feather, mask. None of that anymore. Now, I use just one shampoo. No brush required. I threw mine away, as a matter of fact. But—when I visit my parents to caretake their emergency, I pull out my stash. I've always been a rat, storing away, surreptitious. I don't want my knots to grow enormous and rude.

Now and then, I find a capsule of your euphoria. Without you, my glow is audacious.

The micro-tales collected here were generated from sentences or stanzas that were donated by other writers, but this is not a collaborative project. After the original writer donated their words, they had no additional input or participation. The author thanks all these generous and beautiful writers for their gracious trust in this project.

The author would like to thank the following journals and presses for publishing versions of these pieces: *Atticus Review*, Birds of Lace, The Cupboard Pamphlet, *DeComp, Denver Quarterly, Dusie Magazine, Gulf Coast, LIT, NANO fiction, Pacific Poetry, Paragraphitti, Salt Hill,* and *White Stag*.

Lily Hoang is the author of five books, including *A Bestiary* (finalist for a PEN/USA Creative Non-Fiction Award) and *Changing* (recipient of a PEN/Open Books Award). Her book *Underneath* won the Red Hen Prize for Fiction. She is the director of the MFA in Writing at UC San Diego.

www.ingramcontent.com/pod-product-compliance
Lightning Source LLC
Chambersburg PA
CBHW011430310726
48972CB00011B/3005